Melissa Fitzgerald

Assistant Editor
Leslie Huber, M.A.

Senior Editor
Conni Medina, M.A.Ed.

Editorial Director
Dona Herweck Rice

Editor-in-Chief
Sharon Coan, M.S.Ed.

Editorial Manager
Gisela Lee, M.A.

Creative Director
Lee Aucoin

Illustration Manager
Timothy J. Bradley

Designer
Stephanie Reid

Cover Art and Illustration
Chad Thompson

Publisher
Rachelle Cracchiolo, M.S.Ed.

Teacher Created Materials, Inc.
5301 Oceanus Drive
Huntington Beach, CA 92649
http://www.tcmpub.com

ISBN 978-1-4333-1152-9

Printed in China

Romulus and Remus

Story Summary

Romulus and Remus are the twin children of Rhea, a human princess, and Mars, the Roman god of war. Rhea's father, King Numitor, has lost his throne to his brother, Amulius, who now rules the kingdom. Amulius tries to lock away Rhea so that she will never have children who may take over the kingdom. When Amulius learns of the birth of Romulus and Remus, he orders them to be thrown into the Tiber River and drowned. But Rhea places them in a basket instead and sends them down the river. The babies are found by a she-wolf and a woodpecker, both of which are animals of special importance to Mars.

In time, the boys are found by peasants—a husband and wife. The couple believes that the boys have been abandoned and adopts them as their own children. The boys grow up well, but they have questions about their birth. Their journey to find answers leads to the building of the city of Rome—and to tragedy. What happens? Read the story to find out!

Romulus and Remus

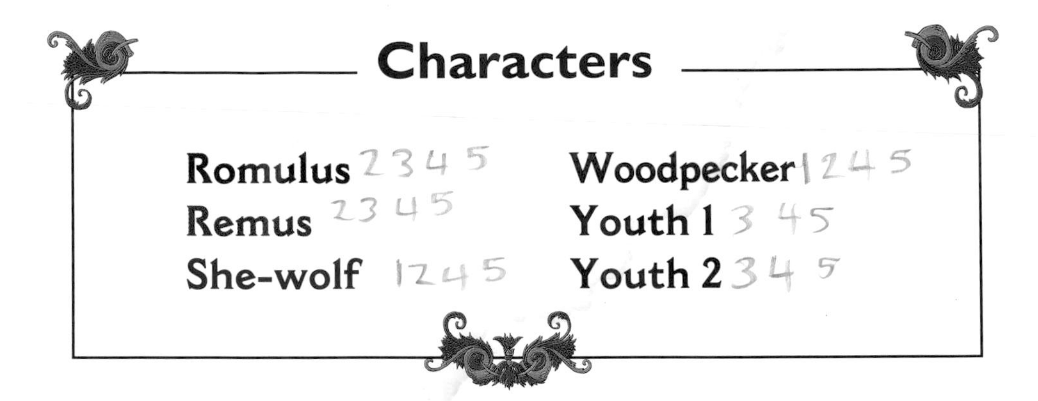

Characters

Romulus	Woodpecker
Remus	Youth 1
She-wolf	Youth 2

Setting

Our story begins on the banks of the Tiber River in the year 771 B.C. The action then moves years ahead, when Romulus and Remus are grown and leave home in search of answers to long-held family secrets.

Act I

She-wolf: Woodpecker, do you hear crying?

Woodpecker: Yes, She-wolf, it sounds like human crying.

She-wolf: It is coming from the banks of the powerful Tiber River. Why . . . it is a human-made basket cradling twin baby boys!

Woodpecker: Holy Zeus! Imagine that. What should we do with them?

She-wolf: They look hungry and frightened. We must feed them and care for them, for that is what the gods would want.

Woodpecker: You are right, She-wolf! I will look for something tasty that humans would like.

She-wolf: And I will feed them some milk to nourish them. Humans like milk, they say.

Woodpecker: Here are some berries for the little ones. How do you suppose they came to be at the river's edge?

She-wolf: There is a terrible rumor among the people that our new king, Amulius, exiled the children of Rhea. In fact, some say he wanted the children dead! And look at the fine clothes they are wrapped in. I believe that the rumor is true!

Woodpecker: No, that cannot be! Who would want to harm innocent children such as these? It is against the laws of nature and of the gods.

She-wolf: It is said that Amulius is afraid for his throne. He will do anything to protect it—even kill his kin.

Woodpecker: Then it is good that we found these youngsters and can keep them safe . . . for now.

Act 2

She-wolf: Woodpecker and I took the babies and raised them as best we could. But one day, when they were playing in the sun near my den, they were discovered by a peasant husband and wife. The couple thought that the boys were abandoned, and having no children of their own, they adopted the twins. Woodpecker and I thought it best that the babies remain with the humans.

Woodpecker: They named the boys Romulus and Remus.

She-wolf: The boys grew tall and strong. But as they grew, so did their questions. They wanted to know who they were.

Woodpecker: And so they left their home to find answers.

Remus: I'm going to miss our home and our parents.

Romulus: I know, Brother. I will also, but we could not stay there forever. There is much we do not know, and neither do our parents.

Remus: I suppose that is true, but how I will miss Mother's cooking!

Romulus: These sweet cakes are the last of it, but we are almost to the river. We can catch some fish for supper.

Song: My Four Little Johnny-Cakes

Woodpecker: These old eyes must be deceiving me! You strapping young men cannot be the wee ones I cared for those many years ago. Lads, what are your names?

Romulus: I am Romulus and this is my brother, Remus.

Woodpecker: Why, you are indeed my little ones! I helped raise you when you both were just babies.

Remus: You? Our parents don't know where we came from.

Woodpecker: Yes, She-wolf and I made sure that you had a safe human home.

Remus: Then you are a friend indeed!

Woodpecker: It was our pleasure. Where are you headed, boys? Are you looking for fortune or maybe an adventure?

Romulus: Adventure is calling us, Woodpecker! We wish to learn where we came from.

Woodpecker: Ah, you wish to hear of your beginnings, do you? Well then, you are in luck, young adventurers, for I know that story well!

Remus: You do? Then please tell us.

Woodpecker: As you wish, but the truth may be hard to swallow.

Romulus: Go on, Woodpecker. We are all friends now.

Woodpecker: You had best sit down for this. Your beginnings are loftier than most. Your birth father is the god Mars, and your birth mother, Rhea, is the daughter of King Numitor of Alba Longa.

Remus: We are of royal blood? See, I told you, Romulus! We are destined for great things.

Romulus: Remus, hush. Woodpecker has important things to tell us. Please go on.

Woodpecker: As I was saying . . . you were banished by King Amulius. Your mother tried to protect you by sending you in a basket down the river. That is how She-wolf and I came to find you.

Remus: You saved us?

Woodpecker: We cared for you before you found a human home. But now that you have grown, you should go back to your roots!

Romulus: Perhaps, you are right, Woodpecker. Maybe it is time to go back home.

Remus: Yes, home. Uh, in which direction would that be, Woodpecker?

Woodpecker: Follow the Tiber River until you reach the large "Welcome to Alba Longa" sign. It is rather hard to miss, dear ones.

Remus: And what will we find when we reach it?

Woodpecker: You will meet King Amulius. He is not a kind man, and you should take care when in his presence.

Romulus: Who is King Amulius? And how did he become king?

Woodpecker: He is a relative of yours! He is your grandfather's younger brother.

Remus: Are you saying we still have relatives left within the city walls?

Woodpecker: You will find that your grandfather, the former king named Numitor, is still in residence. I am unsure of the whereabouts of your dear mother, but try not to think ill of her. She did not wish to be parted from you.

Romulus: But why did you give us away?

Woodpecker: When the humans found you, we knew that we could not care for you as they could. Even though it pained us to part from you, we did what was best. But we have always hoped that we would meet again.

Remus: Where is She-wolf now?

Woodpecker: She is not far from here, but remember that she is more animal than human and would be put off by young men. She may be hard to find. I think it is best if I come with you.

Romulus: Thank you, Woodpecker. Show us the way!

Woodpecker: We traveled for a distance. But then we came to She-wolf's den. She was not there. "Stay here while I scan the forest for her," I told Romulus and Remus.

Romulus: Do you suppose she is hunting for humans?

Remus: Do not joke, Romulus. I hope for our sakes that is not the case.

Romulus: Remus! Look behind you!

She-wolf: How did you get here, young men, and what do you want of me? State your business fast or face the consequences! I do not welcome strangers—unless they smell delicious.

Woodpecker: She-wolf, they mean you no harm. These lads are the same ones that we cared for as babies!

She-wolf: No . . . can it be? Come closer. Why, it is my boys! How I have missed you. How you have changed!

Romulus: We wanted to voice our gratitude to you in person.

Remus: Woodpecker told us how you cared for us.

She-wolf: It is true that we saved you from an ill fate, but we only did what was right. What are your plans now?

Romulus: We have a score to settle with King Amulius. We wish to go back to Alba Longa to confront the king and see our grandfather.

She-wolf: King Amulius is crafty and sly. You both must be wary of him and his advisors, for they have tried to kill you before. Your lives may be in danger again.

Remus: We are ready for the challenges that await us.

Woodpecker: Lads, you will need to be brave, but do not be foolish. Be sure that you are heavily armed when you enter the lion's den, and keep an eye on each other.

Romulus: Do not worry! We have never left each other's side.

Remus: I can vouch for that!

She-wolf: Together is always best, little ones. May the wind guide you safely home and warn you of trouble ahead.

Romulus: Thank you again, Woodpecker and She-wolf. We would not be alive without you, and we are grateful.

Remus: We shall come back when our task is done.

She-wolf: Yes, little ones, set things back to the way they were meant to be. We have always known that you were destined for great things.

Romulus: Farewell, Woodpecker and She-wolf.

Remus: Yes, we will meet again.

She-wolf: Goodbye, dears. Care for one another.

Act 3

Youth 1: Ho there! What do we have here?

Woodpecker: A youth surprised Romulus and Remus and held a knife to Remus's throat!

Remus: Watch the hair, friend. It takes a little work to look this good, you know.

Youth 2: Well, aren't you the fancy one—and awfully calm despite my blade at your throat?

Youth 1: I would not be as concerned with my hair as with whether my head stayed attached to my shoulders.

Romulus: If you unhand my brother, I would be happy to tell you what we are planning.

Youth 1:	All right, but do not attempt anything. My comrades and I have been waiting for some excitement. Now that it's at our fingertips, we are not eager to have it end quickly by being forced to end your lives.
Romulus:	Understood. My brother Remus and I are headed to Alba Longa. We have a twisted family tale to straighten out.
Youth 2:	Hmm . . . family upheaval, huh? That's not unusual for Alba Longa, since King Amulius has made a mess of things.
Youth 1:	He has cut wages and raised taxes, and in doing so, has made life far too challenging for us common folk. But what do you brothers know of hardship?
Youth 2:	Obviously not much. They look strong and healthy enough, and just look at the quality of clothes they are wearing. Their lives have been charmed, I imagine.
Remus:	Looks can be deceiving. My brother and I have a wrong to make right, and our actions may help you in the end.
Youth 1:	What wrong could you make right that would matter to us?
Youth 2:	Choose your words carefully, and do not make promises that you cannot keep.
Romulus:	Amulius took the crown from our grandfather, and we want to see the crown back where it rightfully belongs.

Youth 1: Ah, now *there* is a plot to interest us. It may require more hands than just your four, don't you think?

Youth 2: Luck must be in your favor, for we happen to be part of a rebel gang, and our camp is nearby.

Romulus: I would be very grateful for your help. My only request is that I lead this adventure.

Youth 1: I think we can accommodate that. What are your names, friends?

Romulus: My brother is Remus, and I am Romulus.

Youth 2: What say you then? Do we shake on it?

Remus: Deal. And now that our business is done, do you have something to feast on and maybe a gentle stream close by that I may bathe in?

Romulus: Sorry. My brother often thinks of nothing else but his stomach and his looks.

Youth 1: Right. Come, we have meat roasting on the pit and a cool stream for bathing to your heart's content.

Youth 2: Let us celebrate, for we may have a new king by sundown tomorrow!

Act 4

Woodpecker: Romulus, Remus, and their new friends devised a plan to get past the king's guards, surprise Amulius, and take back the kingdom. They disguised themselves as women, and their plan worked!

Romulus: That was easier than I thought it would be!

Remus: Yeah, good idea! That was genius.

Youth 1: And did you see the look on Amulius's face when he realized who you were?

Romulus: It was priceless. He got what he had coming to him, and now grandfather can rule in peace.

Remus: And it will make all of our lives easier. Woodpecker and She-wolf, what are you doing here?

Woodpecker: The entire forest is buzzing about a pair of brothers and a gang of rogues who defeated Amulius. Tell me, did we hear correctly?

Remus: We only vanquished Amulius hours ago. How could you know already?

She-wolf: News travels fast around here! Did I hear correctly?

Romulus: Yes, we defeated Amulius and reinstated our grandfather as the rightful king.

Woodpecker: That is good news indeed! You have saved us from an uncertain future, and we can be hopeful again.

Youth 1: Not only will the creatures of the forest rejoice—

Youth 2: —but so will the poor folks who have lived and slaved under his rule!

She-wolf: Amulius was a tyrant, and the creatures of the forest were glad to hear that he was defeated. We have had many a bad winter under his rule.

Remus: Now that we have put the kingdom in right order, what will we do?

Romulus: I want to explore the land around Alba Longa.

Remus: Explore? When are we going to settle down?

Romulus: Maybe we will find a place to make our home, but to find that, we must move on.

Remus: But I just found a good barber I liked.

Romulus: We only just got here this morning!

Remus: A good hairdresser is hard to find.

Woodpecker: Maybe you will find what you are searching for where your journey began.

Romulus: What do you mean, Woodpecker?

Woodpecker: Would you like me to show you where She-wolf and I found you and your brother?

Romulus: Yes, let's start there in our quest for a home.

Woodpecker: Then follow me. It is a few days' walk, but with good company, it may feel like a much faster journey.

Poem: The Early Morning

Act 5

Woodpecker: This is the spot where it all began.

She-wolf: And now that we have shown you your beginning, we must say farewell for now.

Woodpecker: Good-bye, lads!

Romulus: So, this is where we might have perished?

Remus: It is not how I pictured it.

Youth 1: It isn't scary.

Youth 2: It's rather pleasant.

Romulus: It is green, lush, and unspoiled. We should settle here.

Remus: Here? Why here? It is in the middle of nowhere.

Romulus: Our story began here. By building a city, we can show Amulius that he holds no power over us.

Remus: He stopped having power over us the day we dethroned him. And anyway, I think it would be best if we settled about a mile downriver.

Romulus: If you would rather be somewhere else, then go.

Remus: Fine! Maybe I will.

Romulus: Fine.

Youth 1: Fine.

Youth 2: Fine.

Woodpecker: The brothers—although never before separated—went their separate ways. While Remus was away, Romulus built a wall to set his city boundaries. Then Remus came back to check his progress.

Youth 1: What shall we call your city, Romulus?

Romulus: We will call it Rome.

Remus: Ha! Rome? A city named after you. How original!

Romulus: Hello, Remus. Have you come back to stay?

Remus: Yes, I've been thinking. I always knew that royalty was in my blood. I shall rule this new city.

Romulus: You? You left! I am building this city.

Remus: Thank you for your hard work, but now it's my turn.

Romulus: I don't think so!

Remus: Step aside, Brother. Just rest while I take it from here.

Romulus: Not on your life! This is *my* city!

Youth 1: What has happened to the two of you? Stop this before you do something you'll regret!

Youth 2: Remember that you are friends and brothers!

Remus: He's no friend of mine!

Romulus: You said it!

Woodpecker: And though it breaks my heart to say it, Romulus picked up a rock in anger and threw it at his brother!

Romulus: What have I done?

Youth 1: You've killed Remus!

Youth 2: Romulus, your brother is dead.

Woodpecker: You are probably shocked by this outcome. So were we all. The brothers who were never apart were now separated forever. Yet despite this tragedy, the great city of Rome was founded on the very spot where their story had begun.

The Early Morning
by Hilaire Belloc

The moon on the one hand, the
dawn on the other;
The moon is my sister, the dawn is
my brother.
The moon on my left and the
dawn on my right—
My brother, good morning; my
sister, good night.

My Four Little Johnny-Cakes

Traditional

Hurrah for the Lachlan, boys, and join me in a cheer;
That's the place to go to make a check every year.
With a toadskin in my pocket, that I borrowed from a friend,
Oh, isn't it nice and cozy to be camping in the bend!

Chorus:
With my little round flour-bag sitting on a stump,
My little tea-and-sugar bag looking nice and plump,
A little fat codfish just off the hook,
And four little johnny-cakes, a credit to the cook.

I have a loaf of bread and some murphies that I shook,
Perhaps a loaf of brownie that I snavelled off the cook,
A nice leg of mutton, just a bit cut off the end,
Oh isn't it nice and jolly to be whaling in the bend!

Chorus

This song has been abridged.

Glossary

banished—sent away from one's country or home

exiled—forced to leave one's country for political reasons

dethroned—removed from a throne or place of power

quest—adventure in which someone is looking for something

loftier—higher in status; superior

murphies—potatoes

perished—died

reinstated—put back into power

rogues—unpleasant characters, possibly outlaws

snavelled—took or stole in a friendly, teasing way

tyrant—a cruel ruler who has complete power

vanquished—totally destroyed

vouch—prove or verify